TWO COOL COYOTES

COYOTES

JILLIAN LUND

DUTTON CHILDREN'S BOOKS • NEW YORK

Library of Congress Cataloging-in-Publication Data
Lund, Jillian.
Two cool coyotes/by Jillian Lund.—1st ed.
p. cm.
Summary: Frank the coyote is sad when his friend Angelina moves away,
but then he finds a new friend when Larry moves into the den next door.
ISBN 0-525-46151-5 (hc)
[1. Friendship—Fiction. 2. Coyote—Fiction.] I. Title.
PZ7.L97882Tw 1999 [E]—dc21 98-50625 CIP AC

Published in the United States 1999 by Dutton Children's Books,
a division of Penguin Putnam Books for Young Readers
345 Hudson Street, New York, New York 10014
http://www.penguinputnam.com/yreaders/index.htm
Designed by Sara Reynolds and Richard Amari
Printed in Hong Kong
First Edition
2 4 6 8 10 9 7 5 3 1